Dear Parents:

Congratulations! Your child is taking the first steps on an exciting journey. The destination? Independent reading.

STEP INTO READING® will help your child get there. The program offers five steps to reading success. Each step includes fun stories and colorful art or photographs. In addition to original fiction and books with favorite characters, there are Step into Reading Non-Fiction Readers, Phonics Readers and Boxed Sets, Sticker Readers, and Comic Readers—a complete literacy program with something to interest every child.

Learning to Read, Step by Step!

Ready to Read   Preschool–Kindergarten
• big type and easy words • rhyme and rhythm • picture clues
For children who know the alphabet and are eager to begin reading.

Reading with Help   Preschool–Grade 1
• basic vocabulary • short sentences • simple stories
For children who recognize familiar words and sound out new words with help.

Reading on Your Own   Grades 1–3
• engaging characters • easy-to-follow plots • popular topics
For children who are ready to read on their own.

Reading Paragraphs   Grades 2–3
• challenging vocabulary • short paragraphs • exciting stories
For newly independent readers who read simple sentences with confidence.

Ready for Chapters   Grades 2–4
• chapters • longer paragraphs • full-color art
For children who want to take the plunge into chapter books but still like colorful pictures.

STEP INTO READING® is designed to give every child a successful reading experience. The grade levels are only guides; children will progress through the steps at their own speed, developing confidence in their reading.

Remember, a lifetime love of reading starts with a single step!

To Susan, who loved the
witch house we made
—C.R.

Text copyright © 2024 by Candice Ransom
Cover art and interior illustrations copyright © 2024 by Ashley Evans

Visit us on the Web!
StepIntoReading.com
rhcbooks.com

Educators and librarians, for a variety of teaching tools, visit us at RHTeachersLibrarians.com

Library of Congress Cataloging-in-Publication Data
Names: Ransom, Candice F., author. | Evans, Ashley, illustrator.
Title: Halloween night! / by Candice Ransom ; illustrated by Ashley Evans.
Description: First edition. | New York : Random House, 2024. | Series: Step into reading |
Audience: Ages 4–6. | Summary: Siblings celebrate Halloween by going trick-or-treating.
Identifiers: LCCN 2023021564 (print) | LCCN 2023021565 (ebook) |
ISBN 978-0-593-80773-6 (trade paperback) | ISBN 978-0-593-80774-3 (library binding) |
ISBN 978-0-593-80775-0 (ebook)
Subjects: CYAC: Stories in rhyme. | Halloween—Fiction. | Costume—Fiction. |
Siblings—Fiction. | LCGFT: Stories in rhyme. | Picture books.
Classification: LCC PZ8.3.R1467 Hal 2024 (print) | LCC PZ8.3.R1467 (ebook) | DDC [E]—dc23

Printed in the United States of America
10 9 8 7 6 5 4 3 2 1
First Edition

STEP INTO READING®

1
STEP
READY TO READ

Halloween Night!

by Candice Ransom

illustrated by Ashley Evans

Random House 🏠 New York

Gobble supper.
Plates are clean!

Time to dress for Halloween!

Orange pj's.

Tiger ears.

Homemade robot.
Cardboard gears.

Lots of kids out
on the street.

Ring the doorbell.

"Trick or treat!"

Silly monster.

"Look at you!"

We get candy.

Say "thank you"!

Costume parade.

Tiger roars!

Superheroes.

Dinosaurs.

Lots of snacks!

Party fun!

Smack the pumpkin.

<u>Crack!</u> I won!

Creepy shadows
on the walls.

18

In the treetops,
hoot owl calls.

21

Big moon rising.

Jet-black cat.

"Eek! What was that?"

Flappy bat!

"I am afraid!
Who went BOO?"
Monster mom!

She got you!

Back at home.

Sorting time!

Candy piles.

Yours and mine.

The night is over.

Time for bed.

Halloween dreams dance in our heads!